Go, Dog. Go!

by P.D. Eastman

HarperCollins *Children's Books*

Trademark of Random House, Inc., HarperCollins Publishers Ltd, Authorised User.

© 1961 by P.D. Eastman
A Beginner Book published by arrangement with Random House Inc., New York, USA
First published in Great Britain in 1965 by William Collins Sons & Co. Ltd.
This edition published in Great Britain in 2006 by HarperCollins Children's Books.
HarperCollins Children's Books is a division of HarperCollins Publishers Ltd,
77-85 Fulham Palace Road, Hammersmith, London W6 8JB.

ISBN-10: 0-00-722546-6
ISBN-13: 978-0-00-722546-0

9 10

The HarperCollins website address is:
www.harpercollins.co.uk

Printed and bound in Hong Kong.

Dog.

Big   dog.

Little dog.

Big dogs and little dogs.

Black and white dogs.

"Hello!"

"Hello!"

8

"Do you like my hat?"

"I

do

not."

"Good-bye!"

"Good-bye!"

One little dog going in.

Three big dogs going out.

A red dog
on a blue tree.

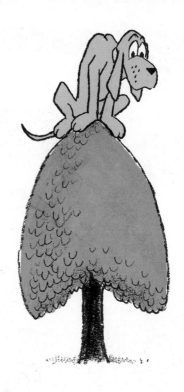

A blue dog
on a red tree.

A green dog

on a yellow tree.

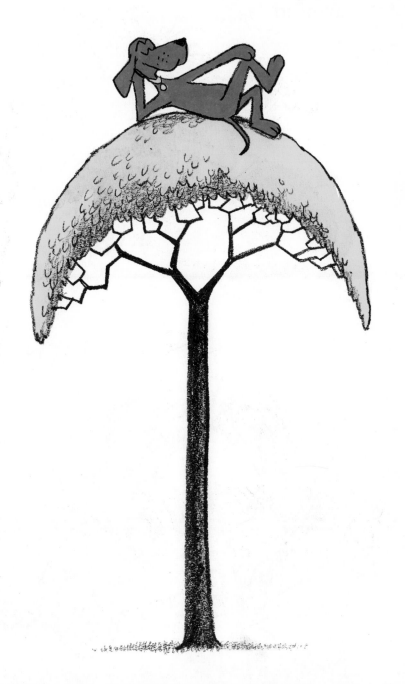

Some big dogs
and some little dogs
going around
in cars.

A dog

out of a car.

Two big dogs
going up.

One little dog
going down.

The green dog
is up.

The yellow dog
is down.

The blue dog
is in.

The red dog
is out.

One dog up
on a house.

Three dogs down
in the water.

A green dog

over a tree.

A yellow dog

under a tree.

Two dogs
in a house
on a boat
in the water.

A dog over the water.

A dog under the water.

"Hello again."

"Hello."

"Do you like my hat?"

"I do not like it."

26

"Good-bye again."

"Good-bye!"

The dogs
are all going
around,
and around,
and around.

"Go around
again!"

The sun is up.

The sun is yellow.

The yellow sun

is over the house.

"It is hot out here in the sun."

"It is not hot here under the house."

Now it is night.

Three dogs
at a party
on a boat
at night.

Dogs at work.

Work, dogs,
work!

34

Dogs at play.

"Play, dogs, play!"

"Hello again."

"Hello."

"Do you
like my hat?"

"I do not
like that hat."

Dogs in cars again.

Going away.

Going away fast.

Look at those dogs go.

Go, dogs. Go!

"Stop, dogs. Stop!
The light is red now."

"Go, dogs. Go!
The light is green now."

Two dogs at play.

At play up on top.

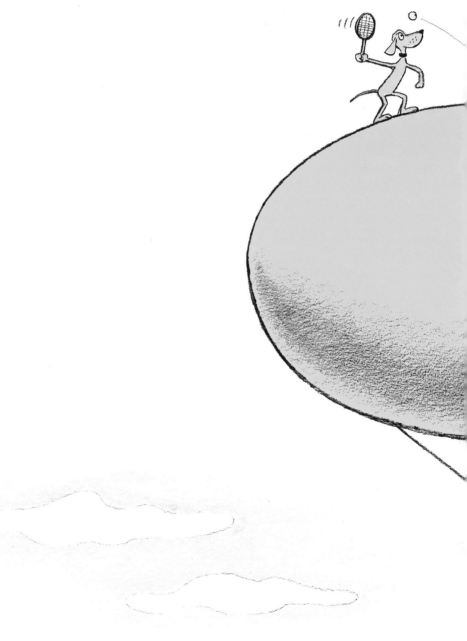

"Go down, dogs.

Do not play up there.

Go down."

Now it is night.

Night is not

a time for play.

It is time for sleep.

The dogs go to sleep.

They will sleep all night.

Now it is day.

The sun is up.

Now is the time

for all dogs to get up.

50

"Get up!"

It is day.

Time to get going.

Go, dogs. Go!

There they go.

Look at those dogs go!

Why are they going fast
in those cars?
What are they going to do?
Where are those dogs going?

Look where they are going.
They are all going to that
big tree over there.

Now the cars stop.
Now all the dogs get out.
And now look where
those dogs are going!

To the tree! To the tree!

Up the tree! Up the tree!

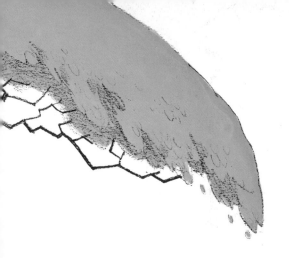

Up they go
to the top of the tree.
Why?
Will they work there?
Will they play there?
What is up there
on top of that tree?

A dog party!
A big dog party!
Big dogs, little dogs,
red dogs, blue dogs,
yellow dogs, green dogs,
black dogs, and white dogs
are all at a dog party!
What a dog party!

"Hello again.
And now
do you
like
my hat?"

"I do.
What a hat!
I like it!
I like
that party hat!"

"Good-bye!"

"Good-bye!"

64

Read them **together**, read them **alone**, read them **aloud** and make **reading fun!**
With over **30 wacky stories** to choose from, now it's **easier** than **ever** to find the
right **Dr. Seuss** books for your child – just let the **back cover colour** guide you!

Blue back books
for sharing with your child

Dr. Seuss' ABC
The Foot Book
Hop on Pop
Mr. Brown Can Moo! Can You?
One Fish, Two Fish, Red Fish, Blue Fish
There's a Wocket in my Pocket!

Green back books
for children just beginning to read on their own

And to Think That I Saw It on Mulberry Street
The Cat in the Hat
The Cat in the Hat Comes Back
Fox in Socks
Green Eggs and Ham
I Can Read With My Eyes Shut!
I Wish That I Had Duck Feet
Marvin K. Mooney Will You Please Go Now!
Oh, Say Can You Say?
Oh, the Thinks You Can Think!
Ten Apples Up on Top
Wacky Wednesday
Hunches in Bunches
Happy Birthday to YOU

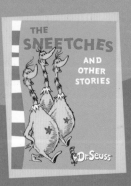

Yellow back books
for fluent readers to enjoy

Daisy-Head Mayzie
Did I Ever Tell You How Lucky You Are?
Dr. Seuss' Sleep Book
Horton Hatches the Egg
Horton Hears a Who!
How the Grinch Stole Christmas!
If I Ran the Circus
If I Ran the Zoo
I Had Trouble in Getting to Solla Sollew
The Lorax
Oh, the Places You'll Go!
On Beyond Zebra
Scrambled Eggs Super!
The Sneetches and other stories
Thidwick the Big-Hearted Moose
Yertle the Turtle and other stories

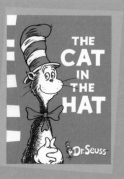